T0196677

The Girl
with the
Magic Vines

AMELIA WARD

THE GIRL WITH THE MAGIC VINES

iUniverse books may be ordered through booksellers or by contacting:

iUniverse
1663 Liberty Drive
Bloomington, IN 47403
www.iuniverse.com
1-800-Authors (1-800-288-4677)

Because of the dynamic nature of the Internet, any web addresses or
links contained in this book may have changed since publication and
may no longer be valid. The views expressed in this work are solely those
of the author and do not necessarily reflect the views of the publisher,
and the publisher hereby disclaims any responsibility for them.

Any people depicted in stock imagery provided by Thinkstock are
models, and such images are being used for illustrative purposes only.
Certain stock imagery © Thinkstock.

ISBN: 978-1-5320-2312-5 (sc)
ISBN: 978-1-5320-2313-2 (e)

Print information available on the last page.

iUniverse rev. date: 06/26/2017

There is no darkness so dense,
so menacing, or so difficult that
it cannot be overcome by light.

VERN P. STANFILL

1

It was midnight. An owl hooted, the wind blew, and thunder crackled. A storm was brewing nearby.

Sage was lying on the bed. Her dirty blond hair flowed all over her pillow as her leaf green eyes drilled a hole into the ceiling. She sighed then, sitting up, surveyed the room. Sage shared her room with twelve other kids, just like they do in every orphanage. The room was dark, musty, and silent.

Everyone else was asleep.

Sage decided to get a fresh breath of air outside, seeing that she wasn't going to get to sleep anytime soon. She sat on a chair on the porch in her brown tee shirt, green vest, and tan shorts.

Suddenly a figure darted across the lawn. The figure was wearing all black. He disappeared out of sight, but Sage could clearly see the bear charging across the lawn, three houses down. On instinct she ran.

The bear was huge and had blood-red eyes. It looked similar to a black bear, but was more of a distorted version of one.

No matter how fast she ran, the bear was faster. Soon,

it caught up with her in a clearing in the forest near Sage's town of Galesboro, Mississippi.

Out here, away from civilization, she didn't have to keep her secret. Sage got a steady footing, positioned her hands in front of her, and concentrated. Vines sprouted, grew, and flowered, trapping the wild animal in the makeshift cage.

Little did she know that the black-dressed figure was watching her. He sat crouched on a tree branch, eyes wide.

He hopped down from the tree effortlessly and approached the creature.

Meanwhile, Sage was still there and her jaw was dropped. Her secret was out.

The person now stood in front of the beast who was thrashing about. He put his hand on its forehead. It somehow managed to panic more. His hand started to glow and so did the bear. Symbols were outlined as the black bear turned from black to white then disappeared.

The figure turned around and removed the hood of his black sweatshirt.

"Hi, I'm Aiden."

2

Aiden was slightly tanned with thick, black, long, floppy hair that covered his eyes a bit. He had three triangles tattooed onto each of his cheeks that made it look like he had been clawed by a wild animal. His eyes were a shade of grayish blue and he wore dog tags around his neck.

"Who are you?" He asked Sage.

"J-just forget you ever saw me."

"Why?"

Sage got in the same position she had to encase the bear earlier. "Try me."

"That's pretty high talk for a-"

Sage jerked her right hand up and vines began to grow. Before they could get a hold on Aiden, though, he jumped up onto a branch that was ten feet up. Sage was in awe.

"H-how d-d-did you-"

He laughed. "I can manipulate air." Just to prove his point further he formed a ball of air in his hands. "I've been tracking that spirit for two months now. I finally caught up with it and sent it on."

"Sent it on?"

Aiden sighed. "That wasn't a normal black bear. It was a dark spirit. I just helped it find light."

"How?"

"I can control animals."

Sage nodded, content with the answer she was given.

"So…what's your name?" He asked again.

"…Sage," she hesitated but managed to say.

"Do you have a last name, Sage?"

"No."

"How do you-" Before he even finished his question, she was gone.

3

Sage sneaked back into the orphanage before any of her roommates woke up. The room was just the way she had left it; dark, musty, and silent. The only difference was that the wind had died down.

She glanced at the clock which said 1:05 a.m. before drifting off into sleep.

Sage woke up with everyone else. She got dressed and made her way to the kitchen. After having her breakfast, she started her walk to school.

Aiden, clad in a friendlier looking outfit comprised of an orange hoodie and dark blue jean shorts, was walking-franticly-around town, looking for Sage. He finally ran into her on her way to school.

"Hi Sage."

She sped up her pace.

"Hello?"

Sage was walking as fast as she could without technically running.

"Sage!" He grabbed her arm.

She flung his hand away.

He got in front of her. "What's wrong?"

"I told you to leave me alone and forget you ever saw me!"

"I'm not a very good listener."

"Tell me about it!"

"Why don't you ever use your powers?"

Sage sighed. "I use my powers a lot but not in public. If my secret got out, I would be put in a cage and dissected… well, probably, anyways…"

"Well…anyways…I was wondering, since…you know…we took down that bear together, if you would help me track down other dark spirits…"

"Um…I can't."

"Why not?"

"J-just leave me alone." Sage then proceeded to walk away, with Aiden on her tail.

4

After school, Sage started the dreadful journey back to the orphanage.

When she was about to open the door, Aiden's surprised voice came from behind her.

"Y-you're an orphan?"

Sage flipped up her hand and a vine grew. It whipped Aiden into a nearby tree. He was able to hear the door slam loudly.

Sage went into her bedroom. Tears welled in her eyes. Luckily she was the first one to get back.

Why did I not tell him? Why did I let him see me use my powers? Why didn't I just stay here last night? Why do I even have powers? Sage thought.

Suddenly, she got an idea. She wiped her eyes and sneaked into the orphanage owner's office. She came face to face with the one thing she wasn't allowed to look through at the orphanage, the records cabinet. Sage found the file on her and went back to her bedroom.

She flipped open the document and read:

Sage, 5/18/03
> *Mother dropped off child. Approximately*
> *30 years old with brown hair and blue eyes.*
> *Vanished. Last seen in London, England.*

Sage was crying happy tears when Aiden came in.

"Sage! What's wrong?"

"Nothing. M-my mom might still be alive."

He hugged her and whispered in her ear, "That's so great."

He took his arms from around her neck and rubbed the back of his nervously. "You know I could help you find her…"

"Yah…but she disappeared in London. How would we even get there?"

"I could get you there," replied Aiden.

"Really? How?"

"I…uh…let's just say I know a couple people."

Sage tackled him in a hug. "Thank you, thank you, thank you! And I thought you were a good-for-nothing lazy trouble-maker." Sage smiled.

5

Aiden dragged Sage through the busy train station. Their train for New York City was about to depart.

"Why are we going to New York City again?"

"I have a buddy that can get us to London." By now Aiden was using his power over air to lightly push people out of their path.

"All aboard!" called the train conductor.

They were less than 20 feet away when the wheels started to turn.

Aiden grabbed sage and jumped, manipulating air to propel them farther.

They landed on the back of the caboose. Onlookers stared in wonder as Aiden and Sage left the station.

Sage and Aiden sat in a seat connected to a table. Aiden flipped out a map that was on a brochure he had grabbed from the ticket office.

He pointed to a harbor in the north eastern section of the city. It was called Amber Port.

"My friend works here. He can get us a boat to London. His name is Rick Amber. His dad runs the place."

"Cool," Sage said. She grew bored quickly and searched the room for any form of entertainment. Sage soon spotted the dessert cart…

She came back with about seven different treats.

"Was that necessary?" asked Aiden.

"Hey. I grew up in an orphanage. The closest thing I got to a treat was an eighth of a chocolate bar."

"Rough."

"Exactly," she said, shoving more treats into her mouth.

6

It was a couple more days before the duo arrived in New York City. When they did, Sage's face was practically glued to the window. Aiden never would have guessed that she hadn't been outside her town at *all*.

That had to have been harsh, thought Aiden.

A little while later, they arrived at the port. Rick met them outside of a warehouse with a gigantic sign that said: Amber Port.

If Rick had to be described with one word, that word would be jock. That's basically what he looked like. He wore a football jersey from his high school of North High. His eyes were a greenish orange and his hair was in short, red curls.

"Hey, long time, no see, buddy," he said to Aiden, "Who's the little lady?"

"This is Sage. She has the power to control plants."

Sage was speechless. He had just blurted her secret and put his own at serious risk.

"Cool. I'll go see what boat you guys can borrow." As soon as Rick left, Sage turned to Aiden and began yelling at him.

"What are you *doing*?! You just spilled my secret! Not just spilled, *blurted* it!"

"Sage, it's okay."

"No it's *not!*"

"His sister can control fire and smoke."

"What? Really? Um…sorry…"

"It's fine. I should have told you about them."

By now, Rick was back, twirling fishing boat keys on his right index finger. They were about to depart when the sky became gray and eerie fog poured in.

"Oh crap," Aiden said.

When some of the fog cleared, Sage could clearly see a figure. He had a slightly tanner complexion than Aiden and the same black, floppy hair except it was messier. He had three small hoop earrings on each ear and the same face tattoos as Aiden, except they were white. His eyes were white too. He wore a white shirt with a black jacket over it. The person had a necklace with a skull and crossbones emblem on his neck, and a creepy, black owl on his shoulder.

"Who's that?" Sage whispered to Aiden.

"My brother," he growled.

7

The black smoke rose as the figure rose its hands. It formed into different animals like lions, foxes, and owls.

Aiden sent a gust of air at his brother. He dodged it and landed on his feet.

"Aww...no 'hello' or 'good to see you, brother'?" He mocked.

"You lost that privilege a long time ago, Hunter."

He smirked, letting one of his fangs show through his evil smile.

Hunter sent a spirit lion at Aiden. Sage made a wall of vines to shield him from the attack.

Hunter immediately took notice of her.

"And who's the little girl, Aiden? Your fan club?"

Aiden just growled in return.

"Fine. Don't answer me," he raised his hands, "but don't say I didn't warn you." His hand launched forward in Aiden and Sage's direction. The dark spirit animals obeyed the command and attacked.

Aiden made an invisible wall of air in self-defense, but this only delayed them. Sage started to attack the ones that made it through. Soon the duo realized they were way outnumbered.

They fled.

Sage looked back to see a black wolf with white eyes and markings running after them.

"You're not going to get away *that* easily," it said.

The wolf is Aiden's brother, Hunter?! She half thought, half panicked.

"Yah, but if you get in your wolf form," Aiden flipped his hand up, "I can control you."

Hunter crashed into one of the warehouse's walls. He turned back into his human form and started to rub the back of his aching neck.

Aiden dragged Sage into the boat and sped off using air to propel the boat as far away as possible.

8

"Explain now," Sage commanded.

"What? I told you already. He's my older brother."

"You can explain better than that."

"Uh. Fine. He can control animals like me. He can also control spirits. He has always been more connected to the spirits," he sighed, "and he used to not be evil."

"How?"

"He's blind you know."

"Blind! Him!"

"He sees through other animals. That's why that owl is on his shoulder."

"Wow."

"Yah…that's also why he is evil. He was a spirit guardian for the light spirits, but one night he was walking in the woods. His owl was gone for some reason and he was attacked by a dark spirit. He couldn't see, so he was easily defeated and turned into a dark spirit himself. That's where he also got his wolf form. He was attacked by the dark spirit of a wolf."

Sage tilted her head in confusion. "Why haven't we seen any *light* spirits? I've seen enough dark ones to last a lifetime."

"They are hidden away so my brother won't find them."

"You do realize that he's not your brother, right?"

"Yah…I keep trying to tell myself that, but it's a different story when he's right in front of me."

9

It took another week for the pair to get to London. Aiden followed as Sage went between shops, excitedly window shopping. He eventually led her to an amateur detective agency.

It almost looked run-down. The wooden planks that made up the exterior were beginning to rot and fall off. The only thing that convinced Sage that it was, in fact, in habited was the light emitting from one window.

"I'll be back in a minute," promised Aiden.

Aiden walked into the detective agency. It was empty except for a 27-year-old working on a computer.

He had long blonde hair and bright blue eyes. He had headphones on. His shirt was light blue and he wore grey capris. Around his neck was a tan hoodie.

Aiden rang a bell that was on his desk. The person removed his headphones and turned around. As soon as he saw Aiden his face lit up.

"Aiden! What are you doing here? Do you have a case for me?"

"Yah, cold case, disappearance," Aiden handed him

the file Sage had stolen from the orphanage. "Can you find something useful, Kevin?"

"You know me. Just a second… and… done!" On his computer monitor was footage from a security camera. A middle-aged woman was fighting Hunter. Aiden tried to make out her face but ultimately failed.

"The video is a very good clue, but it's worthless unless I can see her face clearly."

"You don't need to." Kevin pressed a button on his keyboard and his printer printed an image of the woman. She had short brown hair and blue eyes, just like it said on the file.

"You're a miracle worker man."

"Thanks, anytime." He turned around and put his headphones on, getting back to work. Aiden left.

When Aiden came out, he approached Sage, who had been waiting there patiently. "Good news or bad news?"

"Good news…" she answered, unsure.

"Your mother was here."

"Really?! Wait…what's the bad news?"

"Hunter has her," he growled.

"What would *he* want with her?"

"I…uh…don't know."

"Hmm…okay…so, where to now?"

"Mt. Grey Smoke."

"Why?"

Aiden gritted his teeth.

"Because it's where my brother is."

10

Sage gripped the side of the mountain. Wind whipped her face, threatening to throw her off.

Aiden meanwhile was bounding, rock after rock, up the mountain, moving air to his will.

"Can I have some *help* here?" she yelled up to him.

Within seconds, he was by her side.

"Wow, you really got yourself into a pretty sticky situation."

Sage's arms were in the right places, but her feet could not find a good footing.

"Shut up, Aiden. Some people aren't natural climbers."

"Geez, sorry. You want me to fly you up?" He opened his arms.

Sage took a step towards him, but she chose the wrong place to put her foot. The rocks gave way and she fell…

…or at least, started to. Aiden had managed to grab her and a nearby ledge. He lifted her onto the ledge and said, "That was close."

"To close for my comfort. Oh, and thank you for…you know…saving my life…"

"Oh, uh…you're welcome." Sage could barely see a blush on his cheeks.

Soon, Aiden and Sage were on top of the mountain. They were facing an ancient temple. It was in ruins, but Sage could see faint markings, drawings, and rocks which looked like they had once been statues. On the front of the gateway was a very clear emblem of a moon. It had been painted black, so it stood out next to the bluish gray stone. "Wow…"

"The Temple of the Dark Moon, center of all the dark energy in Europe…and home to my brother…"

"Or what used to be your brother," Sage mumbled under her breath.

11

As Sage entered the building, her heart started pounding and she shivered. It was freezing.

Suddenly a dark cloud appeared and blocked off all the sunlight from outside. Two lions with white eyes formed and attempted to carry Aiden and Sage off.

Sage swung her arm and a vine grew, turning the creature back into fog.

Aiden wasn't as lucky. His air attacks were futile. The lion kept melting back together after being blown apart.

"Sage..." he yelled, his voice fading into nothingness as he was dragged to whom knows where.

"So...your name is Sage...hmm...you're more of a problem than I thought...oh well...this is my element, the dark. You can't see, but I'm used to not seeing and my other senses have adapted to become more powerful. You won't last five seconds," Hunter's voice seemed to come from everywhere.

Echolocation isn't going to help me, thought Sage.

To her surprise, when Hunter attacked, she had a pretty good idea of where he was, and, more importantly, how to attack him.

He transformed into his wolf form and pounced. Sage

could feel the air he displaced and the vibrations in the ground from when he had jumped.

She dodged him gracefully and instantly, her hand rose up, making a vine sprout. As it grew rapidly, the vine hit Hunter in the chest, knocking the air out of him. He hit the stone floor forcefully and went back into his human form. He was out cold.

Just to be safe, Sage wrapped thorny vines around him so he couldn't escape. She went to find Aiden.

Aiden had been dragged to a cellar during the fight. He was shackled to the wall. The creepy white-eyed lion stood evilly smirking, with the keys in his mouth, but it turned to fog and evaporated the moment Hunter had been defeated.

When the creature melted into the fog, the keys dropped from his mouth. Aiden took in a huge breathe of air drawing the keys toward him. Soon the keys were in his mouth. He managed to turn his head and put the keys in the lock. He twisted them and his right hand was free. Aiden then proceeded to use his free hand to unlock his other hand and two feet.

By the time he had done this, Sage had appeared at the entrance to the cellar.

"Sage!" Aiden ran to her and hugged her. She hugged back.

Sage let out a breath she had been holding. "You're okay! Good. You need to do something…"

12

Aiden stood in front of his brother. Hunter was just waking up when Aiden put his hand on his forehead.

He began to thrash his body, but stopped when he realized he was still encased in Sage's thorny vines. He settled for trying to throw Aiden's hand off his head by rocking his head back and forth violently.

It didn't work and soon Aiden's hand began to glow. It was different than with the bear, though. Only patches of him turned white. The patches left his body and formed together into a wolf. The wolf disappeared into nothing and Aiden sat, silently pleading for his brother to be okay.

After several moments of miserable silence, Hunter coughed. Aiden immediately hugged him and nuzzled his face into his brother's neck as Sage made the vines disappear.

"Aiden?" he coughed.

"It's you! I can't believe it's you!"

Hunter hugged him back. "Thank you, Aiden." He turned his focus to Sage. "Hi, Sage."

"Uhh…hi…Hunter…" It was an awkward situation. Two brothers were just reunited and she felt like a third wheel. Not to mention, one of them had just tried to kill her. To make matters even more uncomfortable, Hunter was looking at her with his sightless eyes as though he could actually see her.

The brothers let go of each other and Aiden helped Hunter up. Hunter yelped in pain. Aiden sat him down on a nearby stone bench.

"What's wrong?" asked Aiden.

"Uhh...funny story...just got beat up by your friend when the wolf was in control of me..."

"Oh...um...sorry..." Sage said nervously.

"It's fine."

"Soo...you're going to live? "She asked.

"Oh...yah...I'm fine...can you let me talk to Aiden for a moment?"

"Yah, of course...I'll just...go outside." She shuffled out of the room.

"You didn't tell her, did you?"

"...no...wait? How did you know?"

"If she knew, she would have known that I would be okay. It would hurt a lot, but I wouldn't die."

"I just didn't...want her...to think differently of me."

"You like her."

"What! No! She-I-...-uh fine. I like her. So what? I just want to know if she likes me before I tell her I'm immortal."

"Who is she? Is she an immortal?"

"Maybe...I don't know...she's an orphan, but her mother is still alive...and I think I know who she is..."

Sage sat on the doorstep to the temple. She watched the sun set and the clouds which were tinted to shades of orange and pink.

For the first time that day, the thought of her mother entered her mind. *Where was she? Would Hunter remember what he did with her? And most importantly, what* did *he do with her?* These were the questions that Sage thought of. She immediately wished she hadn't. Tears welled in her eyes.

"Sage. What's wrong?!" Aiden came over and sat next to her. Sage leaned her head on his shoulder.

"Where's my mom?" she inquired.

"I don't know Sage, but I won't stop looking for her, I promise."

Hunter sat cross-legged on a stone pavilion. Sunlight shone on the floor in patches. A light wind blew across him.

Sage and Aiden watched curiously from behind a nearby tree. Hunter's memory from before was fuzzy, so he was going to meditate to clear it.

"I know you two are there," Hunter said suddenly, "I

may be blind, but I'm not deaf. You guys breathe louder than a pack of dogs after running in circles for three hours straight."

"Well, sorry. This is kind of a nerve-racking moment," Sage replied.

Aiden spoke up next, "Yeah and no fair. You're blind. You have extraordinary hearing!"

He smirked. "Okay, but you have to watch from farther than twenty feet away."

Aiden and Sage set off to go watch from the second story of the temple. Hunter could hear them whispering as they left.

"How does he know how far away we are? It's sort of creepy," Sage told Aiden.

"Shh…he has really good hearing. He's probably still listening."

His smirk grew into a full-blown smile. Hunter began again.

The light breeze came and ruffled his hair. He could sense the patches of light around him and the grass coming through cracks in between the stones. The air began to swirl around him. His face tattoos started to glow their white color. The wind picked him up and he started to float.

Then suddenly, it all stopped.

The wind died down to nothing in a split second and his tattoos stopped their glowing.

Hunter stood up, and almost immediately, Sage appeared before him. Aiden was just behind her, panting as he caught up.

"What? What do you remember?!"

"Whoa, calm down Sage. Stop hyperventilating," Hunter told her.

Sage took several deep breaths. "Sorry, I'm just so excited. What did you find?"

"She escaped from me. She was heading towards the village at the bottom of the mountain," Hunter reported.

Aiden gasped.

"What?" asked Sage.

"Remember who lives there." Aiden asked Hunter.

"Who? Who lives there?" asked Sage again.

"Oh no. Not *her*," Hunter said.

"Yes, *her*."

"Who's *her*?!" asked Sage yet again, beginning to get irritated.

"Kya Amber," answered Hunter, "Rick's sister."

14

The village was quaint. There were little red brick houses scattered across the town. There was a small square in the center of the town, made around an old church-like courthouse. The town had a few businesses. All in all, it was very quaint.

Aiden led Sage and Hunter to one of the little red brick houses.

Is it just me or does this house have its own climate, wondered Sage. It seemed to her to be ten degrees warmer here than the rest of the town.

Aiden knocked on the door and a red-haired girl answered it. She was wearing her hair up in a ponytail, but you could still see the natural curl of her hair. She had a black top and light blue jean shorts on. The girl also had a little medallion of a sun around her neck.

As soon as she laid eyes on Hunter she got in a fighting stance.

"Why is *he* here?" she asked, hostility surging through her voice.

Aiden stepped between them. "He's on *our* side now, Kya."

She still didn't seem convinced. "If he's on our side,"

she gestured for Aiden to step out of the way, "What's the one thing I told you *never ever* to repeat to *anyone?*"

"Sorry, I was sworn to secrecy," Hunter replied.

"It's him." Kya got out of her fighting stance and went inside, motioning for the others to follow.

They all went inside and sat on a couch in the living room. Kya spoke first.

"What do you want?" she questioned.

"When was the last time you saw her?" Aiden asked as he handed her a picture.

"Why are you looking for m-" Aiden covered her mouth. "Excuse us," he said to Sage and Hunter. Aiden then dragged Kya into the hallway.

"Why are you looking for Mother Nature?"

"She's Sage's mom. I'm helping her find her. I need you to help me open the spirit channel."

"How did you know she was there?"

"Lucky guess."

The gang was currently walking down a dirt path. For some reason, Aiden was carrying a hose. Meanwhile, Hunter and Kya were on opposite sides of the path and every time Hunter would look over Kya would look away in disgust. Something she didn't know about was going on. Sage decided to ask about it.

"Hi, Kya. What's up with you and Hunter?" she asked, immediately getting to the point.

"Oh, nobody told you?"

"Nope."

"Well…we used to…go out…"

"Really? Let me guess, messy breakup?"

"You don't know the half of it. Let's just say…" she sighed, "I was the first one to meet him after he was attacked."

"Ouch, and he wants to get back together, right?"

"Yah, but I'm not sure if I'm ready."

"Yah, I get that."

"We're here," Aiden announced.

In front of the group of four was a giant doorway. It had three circular holes in it; one in the upper left, one in the upper right, and one in the center. The one in the upper left was outlined in blue. The upper right one was bordered in a red border and finally, the one located in the middle was grey.

Aiden got in front of the middle circle. Kya moved to the right. Aiden handed the hose to Hunter as he passed by on his way to the left.

All at once, Aiden blasted a gust of air into the middle, Kya blasted fire into the right opening, and Hunter used the hose to launch a steady stream of water into the left cavity.

The door slowly opened to reveal a small glade.

16

The small little clearing was dotted with trees and shrubs. A few bushes and trees also surrounded it. And lastly, the path they had been following continued through the door and into the clearing.

Everybody slowly walked into the glade.

Suddenly a small light spirit fox poked his head out of a shrub. It looked around at them, saw Hunter, and ducked back into his bush. Hunter held out his hand and tried to gain the attention of the spirit. It slowly came out of its hiding place and sniffed his hand. Hunter petted the creature and it turned back. The light spirit signaled to its friends that it was okay to come out and several other spirits joined the fox. Each one was a different animal.

After a moment, they continued down the path.

About half a mile down the dirt road, was another small clearing. This one, though, had a small little pavilion. On it was a stone table and it was surrounded by six stone columns.

Everybody stopped and decided to set up camp at that location. Sage decided to take a walk and Aiden left after her, leaving Hunter and Kya alone to awkwardly set up the camp.

"Sage! Wait up!" yelled Aiden. She stopped, but didn't turn around. When Aiden caught up with her, they continued walking. "Okay, there's something I needed to tell you…um…"

"What, Aiden?" Sage said, growing impatient.

"…I…I know who your mother is and where she is…"

17

"What?! I knew you kept secrets from me, but really?! You had to keep my own family mysteries from me when I've been trying to figure them out my entire life!" Sage yelled at the flustered Aiden.

"Look, I'm sorry, but I just wanted to keep the fact that Hunter and I were immortal from you for as long as I could…and if you knew who your mother is, then you would have found out…I'm sorry…"

"So does that mean I'm immortal?"

"Not necessarily. It depends on who your father is. If he's human, you could go either way, but if he's a spirit like your mother, you're most likely immortal. With Kya and Rick, their father is human so only time will tell if they are immortal or not."

"Hmm…Anyways, Who is she?" she asked, getting back to the topic of her mother.

"Mother nature…" answered Aiden.

Sage was silent.

Finally after a whole minute of deathly silence, Sage spoke. "W-where is she?"

She didn't sound angry or all that surprised, just desperate.

But before he could answer her question, a taller than average but not extremely tall woman stepped into the clearing the two had been arguing in. She wore a stylish outfit that comprised of blue jeans and a maroon t-shirt, her extremely long brown hair flowing in the wind.

For a minute, Sage and the woman just stared at each other. That was, until Aiden decided to speed things along.

"Okay, so Eleanor, meet Sage. Sage, this is Eleanor, aka Mother Nature."

Meanwhile back in camp, everything was set up and Hunter was sitting on the stone table while Kya sat next to the fire she had started.

Awkwardness filled the air.

After about five minutes of this, Kya couldn't take it anymore. She sighed and went over to sit next to Hunter. He almost fell off the table in surprise. The light spirit fox readjusted himself between the two. Hunter nervously chuckled.

"Look, I've been thinking and…" she sighed, "I think I might be ready and willing to forgive you."

"R-really?!" Hunter stuttered.

Kya smiled. "Yah…"

Out of the blue, Hunter almost suffocated Kya in a hug. The spirit fox was not pleased with this sudden motion and went to sleep in the tent. "Thank you, Kya," Hunter whispered in her ear.

"And if you still want to go out with-" Kya began.

"Yes."

Kya smirked. "Desperate, huh?"

Suddenly, the sky darkened, the air grew frigid, and black sand started to emerge from nearby bushes. Eventually the sand formed into a large black stag.

"Lennix, leader of the dark spirits." said Hunter menacingly. The stag laughed.

"Good to see you too, Hunter. Just hand over the little nature girl and no one gets hurt."

"No."

"Okay so we're doing this the hard way."

18

Black sand shot towards Hunter, transforming into different animals as it went. Hunter held out his hand in front of him and his eyes started to grow white.

When the stampede of dark spirits hit his hand, they started turning into golden specks of light spirit dust. Only, Hunter couldn't handle the steady stream of darkness coming at him. His footing started to slip.

"Hunter!" Kya yelled.

"Run, Kya!"

"What?! No!"

"Trust me, I'll catch up with you, just *run!*" he yelled back to her. She ran into the forest. The light spirit fox poked its head out of the tent and ran after her.

As soon as they were gone for about ten seconds, he manipulated the spirits to crash head on into a tree to his right.

He ran after Kya.

At a loss of words to say, Sage stared at the woman. She opened her mouth to speak, but nothing came out.

Soon though, to put Sage out of her misery, Eleanor

hugged her. In the middle of the hug, Sage hugged back and Mother Nature whispered in her ear, "I always dreamt I would see you again. I really didn't want to give you to the orphanage, but it was the only way to protect you. I figure Aiden found you?"

"How did you know?" Sage asked, completely baffled.

She smiled, "It used to be his hometown…back in 1874."

"So you really are immortal."

"Yah…" Aiden said looking around awkwardly.

"And you are too, sweetie," Eleanor told Sage.

"Wait, what?"

Before Sage could get an answer, Hunter and Kya burst into the same clearing as them.

"Lennix-is-back," Hunter told them between breaths.

"What?! Wait? Aren't you evil?" asked Sage's mother.

"Long story. He's good now," Aiden responded.

"We need to get out of here," Kya spoke.

"No, we can't. These are the last of the light spirits. We can't let Lennix get them," Eleanor argued.

"Let's split up. I'll go with Sage and Aiden and we'll help get as many light spirits as we can out. Eleanor and Kya can distract Lennix. We'll meet back at Kya's house," Hunter told them. They all agreed and went their separate ways.

19

Aiden, Hunter, and Sage scurried through the forest, leading as many light spirits as they could to safety.

They were close to the door when two streaks of light flashed through the sky. One was red and the other was blue.

"They've...been captured..." Aiden said dismally.

"What?! How do you-?"

"Those streaks show that their power is weakening."

"We have to help them!" exclaimed Sage.

"Yah, we can, Sage. Hunter, stay here. You know why," Aiden said. Hunter nodded.

"Why?" asked Sage.

"He's connected to all the light spirits. We can't risk him."

With that, Sage and Aiden left.

Sage and Aiden peeked through the bushes at the scene before them. Kya and Sage's mother were on the ground, out cold.

Lennix, the black stag, sat on the stone table in the pavilion.

Suddenly, Lennix's evil, black eyes glared directly at them.

"Oh look! Aiden's come to the rescue," it said mockingly. He didn't see Sage yet.

With a wave of his hoof, Lennix had Aiden under his power. He was hovering in the middle of the clearing, unable to move. The stag shoved his hoof which was made of sand through Aiden's chest and it appeared to go through. The sand that made up the hoof started to contaminate Aiden. He could only gasp at the pain.

Sage reacted on instinct, making a vine grow rapidly and slice the leg connected to Aiden in two.

The evil stag's eyes diverted their attention to Sage immediately.

"And he brought a girl," Lennix said in the same tone as before.

Lennix stared at Sage, paralyzing her. Aiden reached towards her from his place on the ground and yelled, "Sage!" Then the pain hit him and he passed out.

Sage was about ready to faint from the stag's power over her when Hunter jumped in between them and took control of the beast.

"Hurry, I can't hold him for long."

20

Sage attempted to grow a vine, but found that she couldn't. No matter how hard she tried, for some reason, the vine wouldn't even sprout.

"He blocked your powers," yelled Hunter as his eyes turned white signaling that his power over Lennix was slipping.

Sage closed her eyes, cleared her mind, and swiped her hand upward. She kept her hand there, but didn't dare open her eyes.

When she finally worked up enough courage, she found herself manipulating water to her will.

Surprised, excited, and feeling powerful, Sage attacked. She used the water from some nearby puddles to surround it around the stag. As quickly as she did this, she froze the water, trapping Lennix.

Hunter went over to the pavilion, took the lid off the stone table, and took out a giant blue crystal. He touched the crystal to the frozen Lennix and the crystal changed color from blue to black.

Lennix was trapped inside, permanently.

21

"Aiden!" yelled Hunter, "Kya!" He knelt down next to them, felt for their pulses, and exhaled loudly, obviously relieved.

Sage went over to her mother. She could see the steady rise and fall of her chest. She was alive.

Suddenly, the light spirit fox came out of a bush and sat next to Eleanor. He nuzzled his nose against hers then continued onto Kya then Aiden. He nuzzled all of their noses.

Sage was confused as to what the spirit was doing, but soon realized when Eleanor began to stir.

He was waking them up.

Everyone was celebrating back at Kya's house. Hunter and Kya were talking at a picnic table. Eleanor figured they were getting back together even though they hadn't mentioned it yet. Aiden was reading a book while leaning against the wall. Mother Nature happened to see the title. It was his favorite book. *He has read that book at least 150 times. Does he have anything else to read?* She also saw several light spirits were romping around, playing tug of war and wrestling. Last, but definitely not least, she spotted Sage sitting on the edge of a ravine, watching the sunset.

Eleanor noticed her and decided this was a good time to talk.

"Hey."

"Hi," Sage replied. She sat down next to her on the edge of the ravine.

"We didn't get to finish our conversation earlier."

"Yah, I was wondering about that… who's my father?" she asked uncomfortably.

"…Father time…"

"Whoa, really?" Sage said, surprised.

"Yah, but he doesn't visit that much. He lives and works on a comet that passes by every 18 years. He doesn't even know about you," she said on the verge of shedding tears.

"Hey, it's okay. The comet will pass by again and then we can both tell him. When's the comet coming? In like, less than a year right? I'm immortal. I'll still be here. It's fine."

Eleanor hugged Sage.

Suddenly, someone coughed behind them. They turned around to see Aiden standing there.

"Can I talk to Sage alone for a second?"

"Sure," Eleanor answered as she got up. Sage could see a faint smile on her face. Something was going on…

"Hey…"

"Hi, Aiden."

"I overheard that you're immortal."

"Yeah, a bit overwhelming if you ask me."

"It gets cooler overtime."

They sat in silence for a moment before Aiden spoke up again.

"Okay look, I've liked you for quite a while and now that I know you're immortal too…will you go out with me? I mean you don't have to. I just thought that-"Aiden started rambling on.

Sage put a finger up to his mouth to silence him.

"That sounds perfect."

Epilogue

While everyone else partied over at Kya's house, a very sinister figure appeared inside the spirit channel. He wore all black and it was nighttime, so it was impossible to tell who it was.

The suspiciously dressed person went over to the pavilion and opened the stone table. He took out the black crystal and disappeared to elsewhere in the world.

Lennix would rise again.

About the Author

Amelia Ward is currently in the eighth grade and a resident of Indiana. She enjoys writing, exploring the outdoors, and anime. Amelia draws inspiration from mythology and folklore.

Printed in the United States
By Bookmasters